LEXINGTON PUBLIC LIBRARY

W9-CPL-075

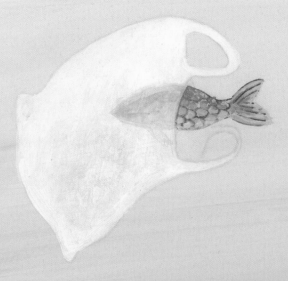

Copyright © 2020 Clavis Publishing Inc., New York

Originally published as *Plasticsoep*
in Belgium and the Netherlands by Clavis Uitgeverij, 2018
English translation from the Dutch by Clavis Publishing Inc., New York

Visit us on the Web at www.clavis-publishing.com.

No part of this publication may be reproduced or stored in a retrieval system,
or transmitted in any form or by any means, electronic, mechanical, photocopying,
recording, or otherwise, without the prior written permission of the publisher,
except in the case of brief quotations embodied in critical articles and reviews.
For information regarding permissions, write to Clavis Publishing, info-US@clavisbooks.com.

Plastic Soup written by Judith Koppens and Andy Engel and illustrated by Nynke Mare Talsma

ISBN 978-1-60537-530-4

This book was printed in April 2020 at Nikara, M. R. Štefánika 858/25, 963 01 Krupina, Slovakia.

First Edition
10 9 8 7 6 5 4 3 2 1

Clavis Publishing supports the First Amendment and celebrates the right to read.

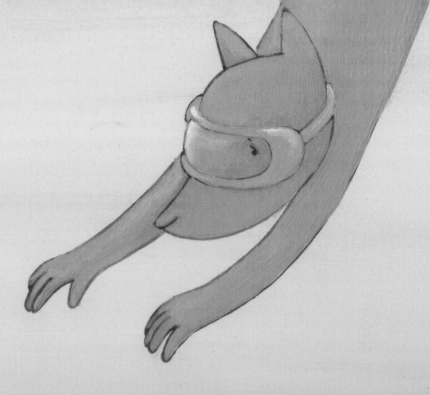

Plastic Soup

Written by Judith Koppens and Andy Engel

Illustrated by Nynke Mare Talsma

Clavis

NEW YORK

Owl, Mouse, and Mole are setting up their spot on the beach.
Here comes the rest of the gang!
"What a perfect day for the beach," says Owl.
"I can't wait to fly my kite," says Mouse.
"But first I'm going to sit and read my book."

Owl, Hedgehog, and Pigeon crowd
under the umbrella with Mouse.
But Frog and Fox are ready to swim!
"Frog, wait for me!" calls Fox as he grabs his floatie.

"Come on," says Frog.
"I'll give you a ride!"

Frog and Fox dive into the water.
When Frog comes up, Fox takes one look and laughs.
"Frog, you look like a sea monster," he says.

"Huh?" says Frog. He reaches for his head
and pulls off a torn plastic bag.
"What is this doing in the ocean?" he asks.

"And this?"
Frog points to a small plastic container.

"And here's a plastic bottle,"
Fox says as he reaches for a bottle
that floats beside him.

Fox and Frog go back to the beach to show
their friends what they found.
"Yuck!" says Mole.
"Double yuck!" agrees Frog.

"I was just reading about that in a magazine,"
Hedgehog says.
"About what?" Fox asks.
"All that plastic in the ocean," says Hedgehog.
"Look, here."
The animals look at the picture in her magazine.
"Much of the plastic that we throw away
ends up in our rivers," adds Hedgehog.
"And since the rivers flow to the ocean,
so does the plastic."
"That can't be good for the animals and
plants that live here," says Mouse.

"Wait," says Frog. "So most of the plastic
that we throw away ends up in our oceans?"
"That's right," Owl nods. "The ocean is like one big plastic soup."

"Yuck, I wouldn't want to eat plastic soup!"
Fox calls out.
"And I don't want to swim in it either!"
"What can we do to help?" asks Mouse.
"Well," Owl sighs, "we should use less plastic.
Because if we don't use it, it won't end up
in our oceans."

Mouse wants to cheer everyone up.
"Let's fly my kite!" she says.
"Yay!" the others agree.
"There's only one problem . . . " says Pigeon.
"I accidentally sat on Mouse's kite."
They can't fly a broken kite. What will they do?

"Wait a minute," Frog suddenly says.
He takes the plastic bag that he found in
the water and begins to tie the kite string to it.
The animals look on curiously.

"It's a kite," yells Mouse happily.
"I want one too," cries Hedgehog.
"Me too," says Fox.
"How about me?" asks Mole.

Frog thinks for a minute and then he has another idea.
"Hey, Pigeon, bring me all the plastic bags we brought
to carry our things to the beach," he calls.
Frog starts dumping the items from the bags into the wheelbarrow.

"Are we going to throw away all the plastic bags?" asks Pigeon in amazement.
"No, of course not!" says Frog.
"We're going to reuse them!"
What a great idea! All the animals join in and help.

"Look, now we can all fly kites," says Owl.
"Plastic kites are better than plastic soup!" adds Frog.
And they all agree.

Do it yourself!

1. Put some paint on a plate.

2. Dip the cork in the paint.

3. Stamp your bag with different colors.